MEM FOX

The MAGIC HAT

Illustrated by TRICIA TUSA

VOYAGER BOOKS
HARCOURT, INC.
Orlando   Austin   New York   San Diego   Toronto   London

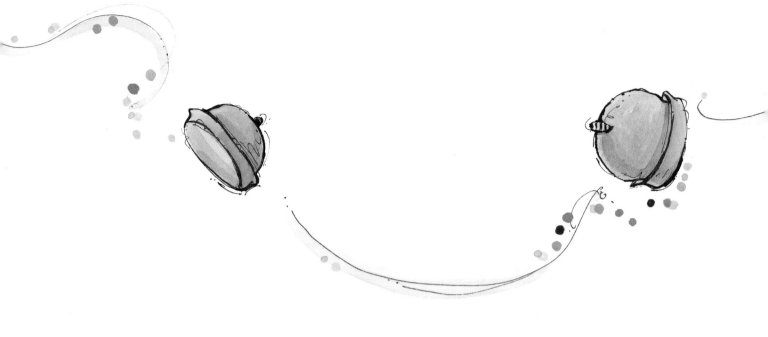

www.HarcourtBooks.com

First Voyager Books edition 2006

Voyager Books is a trademark of Harcourt, Inc., registered in
the United States of America and/or other jurisdictions.

The Library of Congress has cataloged the hardcover edition as follows:
Fox, Mem, 1946–
The magic hat/Mem Fox; illustrated by Tricia Tusa.
p.   cm.
Summary: A wizard's hat blows into town, changing people into different animals
when it lands on their heads.
[1. Magic—Fiction.   2. Wizards—Fiction.   3. Stories in rhyme.]
I. Tusa, Tricia, ill.   II. Title.
PZ8.3.F8245Mag   2002
[E]—dc21   2001001957
ISBN-13: 978-0152-01025-6   ISBN-10: 0-15-201025-4
ISBN-13: 978-0152-05715-2 pb   ISBN-10: 0-15-205715-3 pb

C E G H F D B

The illustrations in this book were done in ink
and watercolor on Arches hot press paper.
The display lettering was created by Judythe Sieck.
The text type was set in Windsor Light.
Color separations by Bright Arts Ltd., Hong Kong
Printed and bound by Tien Wah Press, Singapore
Production supervision by Pascha Gerlinger
Designed by Judythe Sieck

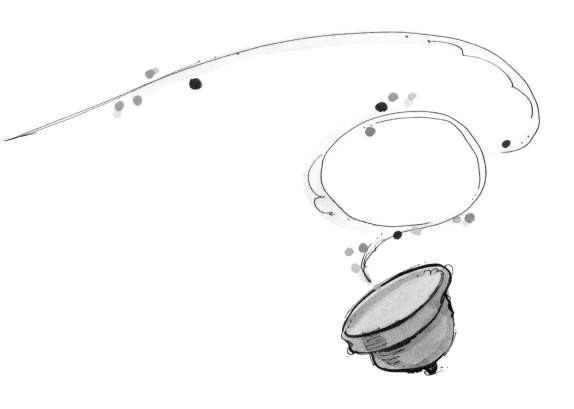

For Mackie and Savanna–M. F.

For Eloise–T. T.

One fine day, from out of town,
and without any warning at all,

There appeared a magic hat.

Oh, the magic hat, the magic hat!
It moved like this, it moved like that!
It spun through the air
And over a road

And sat on the head of a warty old . . .

TOAD!

Oh, the magic hat, the magic hat!
It moved like this, it moved like that!
It spun through the air
Like a bouncing balloon
And sat on the head of a hairy...

BABOON!

Oh, the magic hat, the magic hat!
It moved like this, it moved like that!
It spun through the air
From way over there
And sat on the head of a sleepy old . . .

BEAR!

Oh, the magic hat, the magic hat!
It moved like this, it moved like that!
It spun through the air
(It's true! It's true!)
And sat on the head of a . . .

KANGAROO!

Oh, the magic hat, the magic hat!
It moved like this, it moved like that!
It spun through the air
For a mile and a half
And sat on the head of a lofty . . .

GIRAFFE!

And then . . .

with a skip,

and then

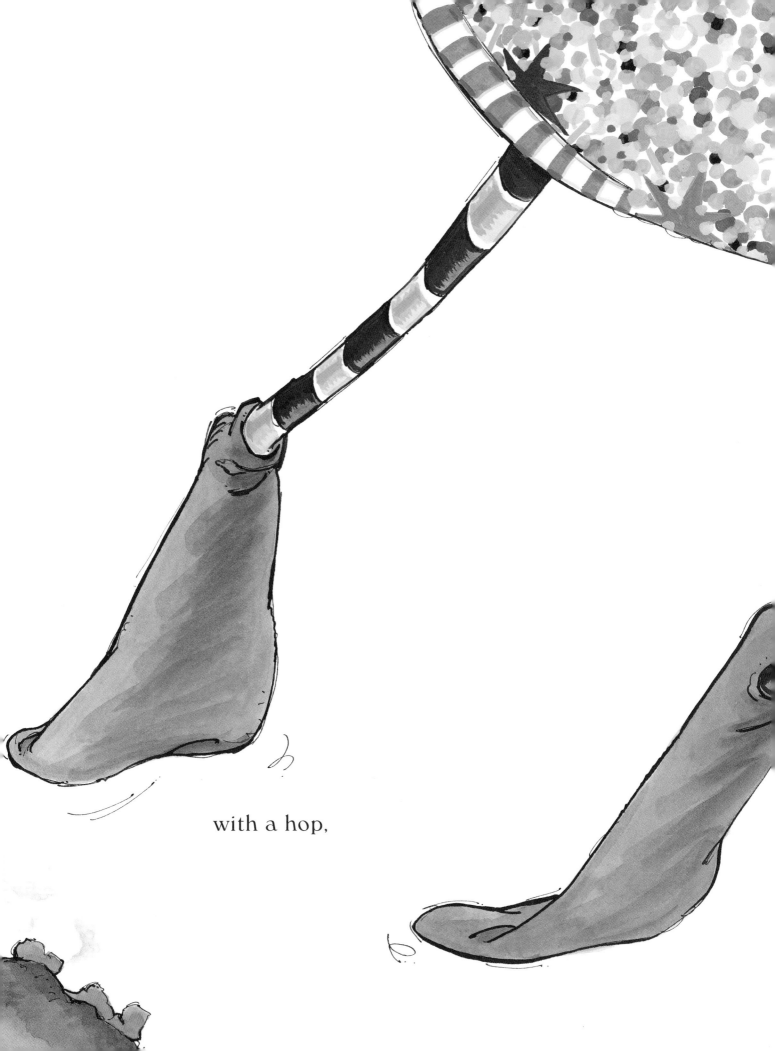

with a hop,

A wizard appeared with a sign that said:

STOP!

So everyone stopped
And stared in surprise
At the wonderful wizard with sparkling eyes,
Who took from his beard, with a nod and a wink,
A wand, which he waved—and what do you think?

The toad, the baboon, the bear, and the 'roo,
And of course the giraffe (Oh, what a to-do!)
Turned back into people, dazed and confused,
Watched by a crowd that was highly amused!

While no one was looking, the wizard, meanwhile,
Skipped out of town with a mischievous smile.

And of course on his head was the fabulous hat

That made all the magic—wherever it sat!